The Chocolate Cow

For Grace Clarke and my daughter, Cristina

The Chocolate Cow

LILIAN OBLIGADO

SIMON & SCHUSTER BOOKS FOR YOUNG READERS

Published by Simon & Schuster

New York • London • Toronto • Sydney • Tokyo • Singapore

"We're going up to the mountains tomorrow. Aren't you glad?" Pierre hugged Melody, his cow. Her big tongue licked Pierre's face. Pierre laughed.

Pierre's father shook his head. "Melody's getting old. She doesn't give enough milk for even one bar of chocolate," he said. "I'll have to sell her in the fall."

"I won't let him sell you," Pierre said, hugging Melody again. "Don't worry."

But Pierre knew his father was right. They couldn't afford to keep a cow that didn't give milk on such a small farm as theirs. Melody chewed her cud as if she didn't have a care in the world.

A few days later Pierre handed his sister, Valerie, one of the cowbells. The family was getting ready for the *poya*, the climb to the mountains. "*Whumf*," she said. "It's heavy."

"That one's for Buttercup," Pierre said. He lifted down another bell. "This one's for Melody."

"I'll miss Melody if Papa sells her," Valerie said. "I love the way she listens to music." Pierre could hardly hear her over the sound of jangling, clanking, and tinkling bells. In Switzerland each animal has its own bell, and each one has a different sound. Even the goats have their own bells.

"I was thinking all night, hoping to find a way to save her," Pierre said. "Let's go. It's time to open the stable doors."

The animals raced toward the sunshine. Valerie ran outside with the bell. Pierre followed with Melody's. He hung the bell around Melody's neck. "You're still the Queen Cow!" he said.

"Valerie! Pierre!" Their grandfather was calling them. "You must help if you want to go." He was sitting on the wagon. Pierre's older brothers, Jean-Luc and François, were loading the cheese kettle. Pierre and Valerie ran over to help.

It was time to go. Pierre kissed his mother and grandmother good-bye. They were staying behind to care for the farm.

Pierre's father turned on a flashlight. One by one the others did too. Soon the procession was on its way. It would go through the towns late at night, when all was dark and quiet.

The last thing Pierre heard was his mother calling "Good luck and good trip."

It would be a long time before he would hear her voice again.

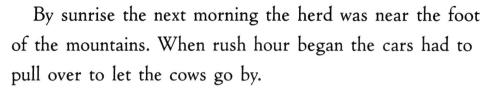

By sunrise the next morning the herd was near the foot
of the mountains. When rush hour began the cars had to
pull over to let the cows go by.

Soon Melody was leading the other cows up a narrow
dirt path. She knew every step of the way, through pine
forests, over old wooden bridges, beside cascading
waterfalls.

Pierre and his brothers walked alongside. Every now
and then they gave the cows some salt. Cows love salt,
and if they licked it they stayed in line. Sometimes one
would stray from the path. The dogs would bark and
force her back into the line.

At last they reached their chalet, high in the mountains. Melody, Buttercup, and the other cows began grazing. Pierre helped his father fix one of the fences. Inside the chalet Valerie set the table. Tonight they would have cheese, bread, and wine for supper. And then right to bed.

The next morning Valerie milked her goats. While his father and brothers milked the cows, Pierre fed the pigs, and grandfather chopped wood. Everyone had a job to do.

After the cows were milked Pierre and his brothers carried the cans into the house. The cheese kettle was hanging over the fire. Pierre poured his milk into the kettle and stayed to watch his father stir it.

"Moo!" It was Melody.

"She wants to see the cheese-making," Pierre said.

"It's the last summer she'll have a chance to," said Pierre's father.

Pierre whispered in Melody's ear. "You can give more milk if you try. All summer long I'll be sure you get the best grass. Please try, Melody. Promise?" Melody licked his face. "Good girl," said Pierre.

One sunny day followed another. The cows and goats ate the fresh grass and grew fatter. Their milk was rich with cream. Big Gruyère cheeses and little goat cheeses sat in molds, ripening. When they were ready Pierre helped his father unmold them. They sent the cheeses to a chalet farther down the mountain, where they would wait until the fall.

Soon the summer was almost over.
Pierre couldn't believe it. One night his
grandfather took out the *cor des alpes*, and
blew some notes. Jean-Luc began to play his
accordion and Valerie her harmonica. François and
Pierre's father began to sing. Pierre began to sing, but
he broke out laughing when he heard Melody singing too.
Still, he was worried. In spite of all the good grass
Melody wasn't giving enough milk.

The next day the good weather broke. It grew dark early. Thunder boomed through the mountains. Lightning crackled in the sky. It began to rain. Big pellets of hail fell everywhere. Pierre grabbed Valerie, and they dashed for the chalet.

When the storm was over Pierre and Valerie went out. The cows were gone! They had been so frightened by the storm they had run every which way.

Pierre called, "Melody, where are you?"

"Buttercup," Valerie shouted. "Come home." One by one, like ghosts, cows appeared out of the fog. But no Melody or Buttercup.

Then, through the heavy wet fog, Pierre heard a clank. He broke into a run and stumbled up the mountain. "Melody! I'm coming!"

"Wait for me," Valerie cried. "Buttercup, where are you?"

Pierre heard Melody moo. She was far away. He ran faster, climbed higher. *Oomph*. Pierre fell back. He'd bumped into something. He felt in front of him. Fur. A tail! He grabbed it. It pulled him along. "It's Melody," he told Valerie.

"She's taking you to Buttercup!" Valerie said. "I know
she is. Listen. Do you hear it?"

The three of them stopped. It was ghostly quiet.
Except for a faint tinkle from another bell.

The fog lifted just enough for Pierre to see that Melody had halted at the top of a precipice. She mooed. Another moo, a weak one, answered her. Pierre crawled to the edge of the cliff. On a ledge below lay Buttercup. She was hurt. "I'll get help," Valerie cried.

It seemed to take forever, but soon the family joined Pierre and Melody. "How will we get her off that ledge?" Pierre asked. He wished they could telephone the mountain rangers, but the chalet had no phone.

"Thank heavens the fog has lifted," Pierre's father said. "The rangers will be patrolling in their helicopter. We will signal them."

When they at last heard the racket of the helicopter, the family sprang into action. François waved a flag, Grandfather played the cor des alpes, Jean-Luc and his father shouted and waved their arms, and Pierre and Valerie jumped up and down. Melody mooed and mooed. The helicopter circled them. "He sees us," cried Pierre.

The pilot threw out a net, which landed on the ledge. Jean-Luc fastened a rope to the cliff and climbed down. He put the net around Buttercup, and when he was ready he signaled the pilot. Up Buttercup went in the net. Then the pilot picked up Jean-Luc. "Will she be all right?" Valerie yelled. Jean-Luc shrugged, and the helicopter flew off with him and Buttercup.

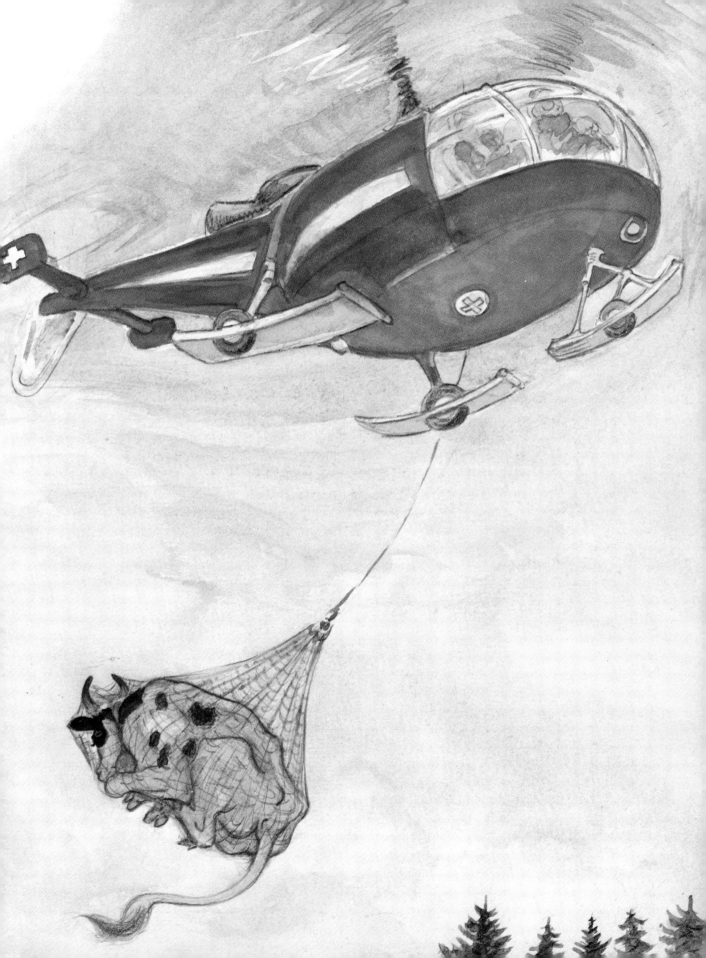

A few days later it was time to go home. All summer long the family had made paper flowers to decorate the cows to thank them for the good milk. Just before they set off Pierre and Valerie tied the flowers and pine branches to milking stools. The biggest headdress would be for the queen. "Who do you think will be queen?" Valerie asked.

"Not Melody," Pierre said. "Even though I gave her the best grass, she still didn't give enough milk."

"And it won't be poor Buttercup. I hope she's all right."

"Is the big headdress ready?" Pierre's father asked.

"I guess so," Pierre answered.

"Good. Come help me put it on Melody."

"Melody?" Pierre and Valerie shouted together. "But you said—" Pierre began.

"I know, I know. But I've never known a braver cow in my life. She risked her life to save Buttercup. She deserves to be queen again."

"Does that mean you're not going to sell her?" Pierre asked. He held Melody's head while his father put the headdress on.

But Pierre's father tied the last knot and only said, "It's time to begin the *désalpe*. We are going down the mountain."

The désalpe, loaded with cheeses, wound down the mountain. Other désalpes joined Pierre's family on the way to town.

The townspeople were waiting. They lined the streets and hung out the windows. It was a happy day for everyone.

"There's Mother," cried Valerie. They ran over to
her. When the hugging and laughing stopped Pierre
began to tell his mother about the storm and the rescue.
"I know all about it," she said. "Here's Melody's
picture in the newspaper. Everyone is talking about her."

As Pierre read how brave Melody had been, his father came up to them. He was with a stranger. "I think Papa found a buyer for Melody already," Valerie whispered to Pierre.

"Oh no," he said. "Not so soon!" The day was no longer so happy.

"This is Mr. Valcourt," said Pierre's father. "He owns the Daisy chocolate factory in the next town. He wants to buy—"

Mr. Valcourt waved the newspaper. "I have been looking for the right chocolate cow for a long time. Your Melody is perfect. I want to use her name and picture in advertisements and on candy bars. I will pay you if you will allow me to photograph your brave cow."

"You mean you want her picture! You don't want to buy her?" Pierre shook Mr. Valcourt's hands. "Valerie! Did you hear? I can keep Melody! She's going to be the chocolate cow!"

"Oh, Papa," Valerie cried. She threw her arms around her father's neck.

The long day was over. Pierre and Valerie walked
home with Melody.

"Something is bothering her," Pierre told Valerie.

"It's Buttercup," she said. "She misses her."

A loud *mooooo* filled the air. "Buttercup!" cried
Valerie. "She's home!"

"Now Melody has her real reward," Pierre said.
He raced after his chocolate cow.

About the Story

Old customs mingle with modern ways in Switzerland, where bustling cities are only a short distance from farms and pastures. The idea for this story came to me when I had to stop my car to let a troop of cows wearing wreaths of pine and flowers pass by. Cowbells were clanging, dogs were barking, and a boy walked along, feeding salt to his cow.

Grass is scarce in the valleys during the summer, and farmers seek better pastures for their dairy herds in the mountains; there the milk is made into cheese. Although some farmers take their animals up by truck, many herd their cows on foot, wearing traditional clothing for the climb *(poya)* and descent *(désalpe)*.

Around Fribourg, in the French-speaking Gruyère region where Pierre and Melody live, people still speak a local *patois*, which has special words for the old ways. Pierre would be called an *armailli*, or cowboy, for example.

Switzerland is also home to many chocolate factories, where milk chocolate is made from local milk and imported cacao beans. - L.O.

Acknowledgments

I am especially grateful to the Jonin family, who were of great help, and to my editor, Olga Litowinsky, who never lost faith.

About the Author and Illustrator

Lilian Obligado was born in Argentina, and spent her childhood there on a ranch, sketching the animals around her—cattle, horses, ostriches, iguanas. She studied painting with a fine artist, but never attended an art school. "I just practiced drawing all my life," she says, "trying to capture movement, expressions, and the atmosphere of places."

She began illustrating children's books while living in the United States and has many to her credit. She now spends most of her time in Switzerland with her husband, a renowned Hungarian historian and genealogist, and their children, Cristina and Sigmond.

 SIMON & SCHUSTER BOOKS FOR YOUNG READERS
Simon & Schuster Building, Rockefeller Center, 1230 Avenue of the Americas, New York, New York 10020

The text of this book is set in Cloister. The display type is set in Parsons.
The illustrations were done in gouache, watercolor and pencil.
Manufactured in the United States of America

10 9 8 7 6 5 4 3 2 1

Library of Congress Cataloging-in-Publication Data
Obligado, Lilian. The chocolate cow / written and illustrated by Lilian Obligado.   p.   cm.   Summary: While spending the summer with his family in the Swiss Alps making cheese, a young boy hopes to find a way to keep his favorite cow from being sold.   [1. Cows—Fiction. 2. Switzerland—Fiction.]   I. Title.   PZ7.O1248Ch   1992   [E]—dc20   91-27464   CIP
ISBN: 0-671-73852-6